DIXIE O'DAY

and the Haunted House

Written by
Shirley Hughes

Illustrated by
Clara Vulliamy

RED FOX

for
Andrea and Ness
with love from
Shirley and
Clara

WEST DUNBARTONSHIRE

D000039896	
Bertrams	29/09/2015
	£6.99
JN	

Contents

. . . and lots more for you to find!

MEET DIXIE and PERCY!

Dixie O'Day and his best friend, Percy, are always ready to go adventuring out. Today we're going to talk to Dixie and Percy about getting out into the Great Outdoors . . . and also about things that go bump in the night!

Hello, Dixie and Percy! We understand you're going to go camping – where would your dream camping holiday be?

DIXIE: *In a remote unknown country – a challenging trek up a mountain perhaps, or into the jungle.*

PERCY: *At the Happy Down Camp Site in a nice comfy caravan!*

What do you pack for your camping holidays?

DIXIE: *I always bring a compass and my especially warm deerstalker hat.*

PERCY: *My 1000-piece jigsaw of 'Scenes from Didsworth' and plenty of chocolate buttons.*

And what do you like to do on your camping trips?

DIXIE: *I like to do my morning exercises in the fresh air, and build a campfire.*

PERCY: *And I entertain with some campfire songs on my ukulele.*

What's your top camping tip?

DIXIE: *Take lots of spare socks – you will need them to keep your feet warm at night.*

PERCY: *Check the weather forecast before you set out.*
Do you believe in ghosts?
DIXIE: *No, it's just your imagination playing tricks on you.*
PERCY: *Ooh, I'm not so sure . . .*
Can you tell us what kind of things give you the spooks?
PERCY: *Ghosts, ghouls, witches, werewolves, vampires, skeletons, lightning, creepy crawlies – oh dear, almost EVERYTHING!*
DIXIE: *My neighbour, Lou Ella!*
What do you do when you're feeling a bit frightened?
PERCY: *I cling on to Dixie!*
DIXIE: *I try to reassure Percy.*

Thank you, Dixie and Percy – and have a lovely trip!

Lou Ella
likes:
Fast cars
Expensive holidays
Ruining Dixie and
Percy's fun

**The
Friendly Family**
likes:
Camping
Playing games
Baked beans on toast

Margery
and Mabel
like:

Grass

Bob Beck
likes:
Taking good care of things

Mrs Arkwright
likes:

Her house

Chapter One

DIXIE O'DAY

Dixie was planning a camping holiday and he invited his friend Percy to join him.

and the Haunted House

'What we need is the simple life, Percy!' he said.

Cuckoo!

DIXIE O'DAY

'We won't go to a camp site with all those cafés and table tennis and showers with hot running water. We'll go somewhere where there are no other people and we can be alone with nature!'

'Sounds great,' Percy agreed. But he added: 'Nothing wrong with a nice hot shower, though!'

DiXiE O'DAY

On the morning of their departure Dixie got up very early. After a quick breakfast he began packing the boot of his car with a small tent,

two sleeping bags and groundsheets,

a portable cooking stove

and a few basic provisions.

and the Haunted House

It was some time before Percy arrived. He was loaded down with all sorts of things, including jigsaws, a radio, puzzles, his ukulele and plenty of chocolate.

DIXIE O'DAY

'Surely we don't need all that,' said Dixie. 'This is supposed to be the simple life, remember?'

But Percy firmly stowed them aboard.

Dixie's nosy neighbour Lou Ella had come to her front gate to watch. 'I hope the weather stays fine for you,' she said. 'The forecast on the radio said it was going to rain later.'

DIXIE O'DAY

Dixie and Percy ignored her. She was still standing there watching them as they drove off.

They drove for several hours with Dixie at the wheel. Percy read the road map.

and the Haunted House

DIXIE 1

DIXIE O'DAY

At last they left the main road behind and reached some beautiful open countryside.

They saw a sign pointing to the Happy Down Camp Site, but Dixie sped past.

As they did so, Percy caught a glimpse of the friendly family.

There was Mum, Dad and the
three little ones, settling down in
their comfortable camping trailer,
with hot showers near at hand, and
a shop in case they needed extra
supplies. He felt a small pang of envy.

But Dixie kept going, and soon they turned into a winding lane with high hedges on either side.

They passed only one house, a very old one, set well back from the lane behind unkempt bushes.

It looked rather ramshackle, and its uncurtained windows looked out blankly from beneath a tumbledown roof.

DIXIE O'DAY

'I don't much like the look
of that place,' said Percy.
'Doesn't seem like there's
anyone living there. It's a
bit spooky, if you ask me.'

They kept going for a long time, until at last Dixie stopped the car by a five-barred gate. They both got out and peered over it into the field beyond.

'This looks just right,' said Dixie enthusiastically. 'I do believe there's a stream down there by those trees. It's an ideal spot!'

Right away he scrambled through a hole in the hedge.

'You begin unpacking the car, Percy,' he called back. 'And I'll pile our things up on this side. Then we'll pick out a really good place to pitch our tent.'

DiXiE O'DAY

Neither of them had noticed the sign near the gate which read:

**STRICTLY PRIVATE —
KEEP OUT!
TRESPASSERS WILL BE
PROSECUTED**

Chapter Two

DIXIE O'DAY

It took them quite a long time to get everything through the hedge and into the field. When they had finished, Percy was feeling rather tired.

'It's well past lunch time,' he said forlornly. 'Do you think we could eat our picnic first, before we put up the tent?'

'Well, I suppose so,' said Dixie. 'I'm a bit peckish myself. But we must save some of our supplies for supper.'

Percy was already worrying about what they were going to eat for breakfast the next morning.

It was too muddy to sit down, so they ate standing up.

DiXiE O'DAY

Then Dixie looked around for exactly the right spot to pitch their tent. At last they settled on a gentle slope not far from the stream.

Putting up the tent was more difficult than they had thought.

When they
had finished,
it leaned over
sideways a bit.
But they laid
their sleeping

bags and other belongings carefully
inside, then got busy gathering wood
for the campfire.

Percy found two big logs for them to sit on.

'Marvellous!' said Dixie. 'Well done, Percy! This is quite like home! Now let's go for a dip in the stream before it gets dark.'

Some distance away, at the top of the field, two cows, Mabel and Margery, watched them as they stripped off to their vest and pants and picked their way down to the stream.

DIXIE O'DAY

'Not the best choice of a place to swim,' said Mabel, chewing thoughtfully. 'It was very sticky under-hoof when we were down there this morning.'

'I hope they manage to avoid the brambles,' said Margery. 'Shall we wander over while they're having their bathe and take a look at their tent?'

The stream was overhung with trees. Dixie was the first to jump in.

It was lucky he did not dive because the water was only knee deep.

DIXIE O'DAY

Percy followed, very gingerly. The
mud squelched up between his toes.
Dixie struck out at once into the
deeper water.

'Come on in, Percy!' he called
back. 'It's not so cold once you get in!'
'It's a bit smelly, isn't it?' said
Percy.

He dithered for some minutes,
hugging himself doubtfully, before
he took the plunge. Then, swimming
a cautious breast-stroke, he followed
Dixie upstream.

DIXIE O'DAY

Meanwhile, Mabel and Margery were having an interesting time examining the camp site.

They nosed through some of the provisions and managed to upset the carefully laid campfire. Then they peered into the tent.

'Better not go too far inside,' said
Mabel. 'It doesn't look very secure.'

'No,' said Margery. 'Or waterproof,
either. And it's going to rain tonight,
I'm afraid.' As she was a cow, she
knew this for certain.

DIXIE O'DAY

Dixie and Percy did not stay in the water for very long. As they waded back through the weeds towards the bank, they stumbled over brambles half hidden in the water.

Luckily neither of them was hurt, but Dixie's underpants suffered an inconvenient tear.

They were both in a bad mood as they made their way back to their camp. When they saw the mess that Mabel and Margery had made, Dixie was very cross.

DiXiE O'DAY

'Cows!' he shouted. 'Just look at all the mess they've made with their big stomping hoofs!'

Percy was equally annoyed. But he thought it wiser not to point out that the cows probably had more right to be in this field than they did.

'We'll have to build our campfire all over again before we can get properly warm,' he said, shivering.

DIXIE O'DAY

'Thank goodness we brought the cooking stove! It'll be dark soon.' He glanced nervously at the shadows lengthening over the field.

Chapter Three

DIXIE O'DAY

When they had got the fire going, they dried themselves, brewed up a hot drink, then cooked a supper of baked beans and sausages.

Afterwards Percy played Dixie
a couple of tunes on his ukulele
to cheer him up.

But a brisk wind had got up, and
was blowing strongly. The tent flapped
and the sky darkened.

Percy was just about to suggest they do a jigsaw when the rain started: great gusts of it sweeping across the field. They hurried inside the tent.

'Time to go to bed, I suppose,' said Dixie gloomily.

'But it's only seven thirty!' Percy objected. He searched in his rucksack for a book to read.

Unfortunately, the only one he had brought with him was called *Ghosts, Ghouls and Other Real Life Hauntings* by Winifred Beazley.

He started off reading aloud by torchlight, but his voice became more and more squeaky with terror. In the end he snapped the book shut.

DiXiE O'DAY

'Perhaps we'd better try to sleep,'
said Dixie. 'We'll get up early tomorrow.
The rain may have cleared up by then.'

As they huddled down into their
sleeping bags, they could hear the rain
driving hard against the roof of the
tent. Percy lay there, staring into the
darkness. He knew that, a few inches
away from him, Dixie was awake too.

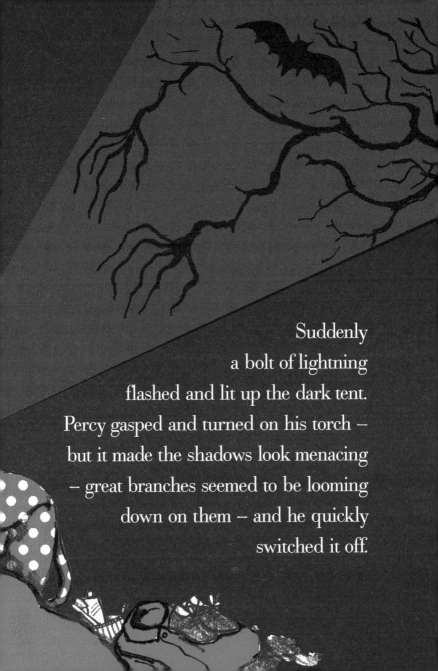

Suddenly
a bolt of lightning
flashed and lit up the dark tent.
Percy gasped and turned on his torch –
but it made the shadows look menacing
– great branches seemed to be looming
down on them – and he quickly
switched it off.

DIXIE O'DAY

'I don't like this,' he whispered.
It felt very dark and lonely inside the
tent, with the rain beating down, owls
hooting, and blasts of cold wind coming
in under the flap.

All at once there came an extra
strong gust of wind. The tent rocked
dangerously and lurched sideways.

There was another huge gust, and one whole side collapsed inwards on top of them, bringing a torrent of rainwater with it.

DIXIE O'DAY

They staggered to their feet and dragged on their clothes.

'We'll have to get back to the car!' shouted Dixie. 'Bring what you can!'

They abandoned the tent and struggled to the gate with as many of their belongings as they could manage.

DIXIE O'DAY

When they were safely inside the car, they sat there for some time without speaking.

'Home?' said Dixie at last.

'Home!' agreed Percy firmly.

Chapter Four

DIXIE O'DAY

Dixie turned the key in the ignition.
The engine stuttered for a moment,
then died.

He turned the key again,
but the same thing
happened.

He tried the accelerator
several times. Still nothing.

'That's funny,' he said. 'I've never known her behave like this before.'

Then Percy pointed silently to the petrol gauge. It was at EMPTY. There was a brief pause, broken only by the sound of the driving rain on the windscreen.

DIXIE O'DAY

'Oh dear,' said Dixie. 'I think I must have forgotten to fill her up before we left Didsworth.'

'What are we going to do? Where are we going to sleep?' muttered Percy nervously. He didn't like being out in the countryside at night. It was much darker than in Didsworth. He'd had quite enough of the outdoor life.

and the Haunted House

But Dixie was peering out into the
rain-washed darkness. 'Look, Percy!
Let's try that farmhouse at the top of
the hill – I'm sure they'll be willing to
help us out!'

DiXiE O'DAY

Dixie and Percy trudged through the mud, up to the farmhouse door. But when they knocked, it was only opened a crack and they were not given a warm welcome by the farmer, who was already in his pyjamas.

'Didn't you read the sign? Trespassers will be prosecuted! This is my land – now hop it . . .'

'But . . . ?' squeaked Percy.

However, the farmer had already slammed the door.

'What a mean, unhelpful fellow,' said Percy, feeling very discouraged.

Dixie, meanwhile, was scanning the horizon for any other signs of life.

DIXIE O'DAY

'Wait a minute, Percy. I think I can see a light in that old house we passed in the lane. There must be someone living there after all! Surely they can help us.'

They could see a faint light glimmering in the downstairs windows. The big front gate stood slightly open.

DIXIE O'DAY

'Looks as though there's someone at home, anyway,' said Dixie.

'I do hope they're not hostile to strangers!' muttered Percy.

'We'll have to give it a try now we've got this far – come on!' said Dixie.

There was no doorbell, only a strange old-fashioned doorknocker in the shape of a grinning face. Dixie knocked.

No one answered. He knocked again, several times. The sound echoed through the house, but nobody stirred within. The cold rain was still coming down relentlessly, making their teeth chatter.

DIXIE O'DAY

In desperation, Dixie tried the door. It creaked open.

'We can't just walk in!' squeaked Percy.

But Dixie was already leading the way inside.

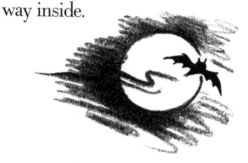

Chapter Five

DIXIE O'DAY

They stepped into a tall entrance
hall with a wide wooden staircase.
Everywhere, on massive chests and
tables, stood candelabras with candles
all alight. Their two shadows leaped up
against the panelled walls.

Dixie cleared his throat. 'Hello? Sorry to barge in like this, we were wondering if you could help us . . .' His words echoed up to the high ceiling, but there was no answer.

They peered through a half-open
doorway into a large reception room,
but everything was shrouded in dust
sheets. Large anonymous objects
loomed up, throwing grotesque
shadows onto the ceiling. Silently they
withdrew and closed the door.

At the back of the hall, as though guarding the foot of the stairs, stood a suit of armour.

'Don't let's go near!' squeaked Percy.

But Dixie could not resist opening the visor of the helmet and peering inside.

For a moment he thought he saw two sharp eyes peering back at him. But then they disappeared. He hastily snapped it shut.

It was then that
they heard a faint movement on the
dark upstairs landing. A small figure
appeared at the top of the stairs, half
hidden in the shadows, beckoning.

DIXIE O'DAY

It seemed to be a little old lady.
Dixie launched into another fulsome
apology. He could feel Percy clutching
the back of his jacket.

The old lady did not reply. She simply
smiled and beckoned them upstairs.
There seemed to be no alternative but
to follow her. But when they reached
the landing, she had disappeared.

Ahead of them was a long passage lit
by more flickering candles. Very
cautiously they made their way along it.
On the walls hung framed portraits
of elaborately dressed ladies and
gentlemen from another era, long ago.

DiXiE O'DAY

As they edged past, Dixie and Percy both had the very uncomfortable feeling that the eyes of the paintings were following them, watching their every move. Or was it just a trick of the light?

Chapter Six

All at once they glimpsed the old
lady again, hovering at the end of the
passage, still smiling and pointing the
way. They hurried on, and when they
reached her, she gestured to an open
door. They stepped inside, and she
closed it softly behind them.

and the Haunted House

'I don't like this!' squeaked Percy.
His voice did not seem to be
functioning properly.

DIXIE O'DAY

Dixie and Percy looked around.
They were in a large, comfortable room
with a fire burning in the grate, and
two armchairs drawn up beside it.
There was a huge four-poster bed with
the curtains pulled back. It was a
tempting sight.

They sat down on it for a moment to
rest. A faint cloud of dust rose from it
but it did not seem too damp.

'I'm just SO tired,' murmured Dixie.

'Me too,' Percy agreed.

DiXiE O'DAY

The warmth from the fire seemed to make it difficult to move. They half expected the old lady to come peeping round the door, but the house was now completely silent.

And somehow, before they realized what they were doing, they had both kicked off their shoes and sunk down onto the bed. Then, pulling the curtains tightly around them, they huddled under the quilt and fell into a deep sleep.

DIXIE O'DAY

When Percy opened his eyes, it was
pitch dark. At first he couldn't
remember where he was. Something
had woken him. It certainly wasn't
Dixie's snores.

and the Haunted House

He squinted at his watch: 4.30 a.m.
He lay there, tense, listening. It was
when the curtains of the old
four-poster stirred slightly that he
knew that somebody else was in the
room. His throat was too dry to
call out. And, anyway, he was
too terrified of getting
an answer.

DIXIE O'DAY

Percy clutched Dixie and shook
him awake.

'Wasser masser? What's up?'
he muttered. But Percy
put his hand over
Dixie's mouth.

Perhaps it was
the little old lady.
But it did not sound
like her. Whoever it was,
he or she was now prowling
about the room. They lay there,
clinging together, as the footsteps
began to circle the bed. Then the
curtains were suddenly jerked back!
Dixie and Percy cowered under the
quilt, dazzled by the torch that was
shining into their faces . . .

DIXIE O'DAY

'Who's there?' said a voice.

Chapter Seven

DIXIE O'DAY

At first light, when the rain had stopped at last, Dixie and Percy found themselves sitting in front of another fire, this time a sensible electric one.

'Pity you didn't try my house first,' said Bob Beck as he handed them each a cup of tea.

and the Haunted House

He was the caretaker of the old house they had so foolishly entered the night before. He and his wife lived in a modern bungalow situated at the back, away from the drive. If it had not been so dark, Dixie and Percy might easily have found it.

'Out of petrol, were you?' said Bob.

DiXiE O'DAY

'Gave me quite a shock, finding you there. The rain woke me, so I thought I'd better go and check that the leak I'd mended in the roof was holding up all right. Funny the front door was open, though. I could have sworn I'd locked up last night as I always do.'

'We should not have intruded, of course,' said Dixie. 'It was quite wrong of us. And naturally we would not have done so if the lady of the house had not beckoned us upstairs. What is her name, by the way? We must thank her.'

'The lady?'

DIXIE O'DAY

'Yes – we didn't actually speak to her, but she seemed most welcoming.'

Bob paused. 'Oh, that lady. That would be old Mrs Arkwright.'

and the Haunted House

'She's the owner of the house, I presume,' said Dixie.

'Well, yes. Or rather she was. You see, she *died nearly fifty years ago*.'

'But it CAN'T have been a ghost!' said
Dixie. 'I simply don't believe in them!'

They were back in the car and on
their way home, with plenty of petrol in
the tank, helpfully supplied by Bob.

'Neither do I,' said Percy. 'At least, I
don't think so.'

'Well,' said Dixie, 'if she was a ghost,
she wasn't very frightening. She seemed
pretty friendly to me.'

But much about the night they had spent in the old dark house remained unexplained.

Particularly the fact that, when Bob had shown them around again that morning before they left, they found no candles anywhere, and the fire in the bedroom grate had clearly not been lit for a very long time.

DIXIE O'DAY

Dixie and Percy drove on in silence for a while. But when they reached the main road, thoughts of that old dark house and the terrors of the night seemed to fade rapidly.

'Pity about your tent,' said Percy at last.

Dixie laughed. 'Drat the tent,' he said. 'If the weather looks up next weekend, we could have a barbecue in my back garden. Bring your ukulele . . .

. . . That at least will give Lou Ella something to complain about!'

Shirley is Clara's mum, and together they have created Dixie and Percy's adventures. Let's find out more about them!

Hello, Shirley and Clara!

What do you pack for your camping holidays?

Shirley: A luxurious sleeping bag and a reliable torch.

Clara: A stove and plenty of delicious food for breakfast – eggs, beans, fried bread and tomato sauce!

What's your top camping tip?

Shirley: Make sure your tent has no leaks!

Clara: Don't forget marshmallows for the campfire.

Do you believe in ghosts?

Shirley: Not in daylight . . .

Clara: I saw a ghost once, when I was about five – at least I thought I did. It still gives me the shivers to think about it.

Can you tell us what kinds of things give you the spooks?

Shirley: Thinking I hear a knock at the door and finding nobody there.

Clara: The noise of branches on the windowpane and the wind whistling in the chimney.

What do you do when you're feeling a bit frightened?

Shirley: I get into bed and pull the blanket over my head!

Clara: And I jump in too!

Thank you for sharing your spooky stories with us, Shirley and Clara!

There are ten differences between these two pictures – can you spot them all? *(Answers on the next page.)*

Draw Your Own Portrait!

Percy sees lots of portraits in the spooky house. Can you draw your own?

First, draw a picture frame. Now fill it in with a picture of yourself, or of somebody else. What kind of clothes are you wearing? What else would you like to include in the picture?

When you've come up with your portrait, go to

www.dixieoday.com

to find out how to send it to Dixie!

Answers to Spot the Difference

1. Percy's pocket is missing   2. One of Dixie's buttons is missing   3. Dixie's hat has changed colour.   4. There is a missing tree branch.   5. The lamp has changed colour.   6. There is a missing window.   7. A window has changed colour.   8. There is a missing chimney pot.   9. A bat has been added.   10. A bat has changed colour.

The Dixie O'Day Quiz

Dixie has written a special quiz to test you! How much can you remember about *Dixie O'Day and the Haunted House?*

I. True or false: Percy brings a trumpet on the camping trip.

2. Who reads the map on the journey?

3. Who is camping at the Happy Down Camp Site?

4. What are the cows called?

5. True or false: Dixie and Percy go swimming.

6. Who makes a mess of their Camp Site?

7. What do Dixie and Percy have for dinner?

8. Who wrote *Ghosts, Ghouls and Other Real Life Hauntings*?

9. True or false: Dixie's car has run out of petrol?

IO. Who slams the door on Dixie and Percy?

II. What is Bob Beck's job?

I2. Where does Bob Beck live?

ANSWERS

1 False – he brings a ukulele   2 Percy   3 The Friendly Family   4 Mabel and Margery   5 True   6 Mabel and Margery   7 Baked beans and sausages   8 Winifred Beazley   9 True   10 The farmer   11 Caretaker of the old house   12 In a bungalow behind the old house

If you enjoyed

DIXIE O'DAY
and the Haunted House,

then you'll love Dixie and Percy's

next adventure

DIXIE O'DAY
On His Bike!

Read on for the first chapter . . .

DIXIE O'DAY
On His Bike!

Chapter One

One fine morning, when Dixie O'Day's friend Percy had come over to help him wash his car, a cyclist passed by. He slowed down, dismounted, and stood watching them for a while. Then he said, in a friendly way:

'That's a lovely vehicle you have there. And you keep it in

very good condition, I see.'

Dixie was pleased. He stood back, sponge in hand, to admire the sparkle on the windscreen.

'Thanks,' he said. 'She's not the latest model exactly, but she goes beautifully. Never had any trouble with the engine. Well, hardly ever. But I see you are a cyclist yourself.'

'Yes – I love it. Go off on lots of long rides at weekends. I'm staying here in Didsworth with my auntie at the moment. Exploring the area a bit on my bike.'

'This is my friend Percy,' said Dixie. 'We were just thinking of

having a coffee break. Would you care for a cup?'

The cyclist introduced himself as Dean Delaney, and soon he and Dixie were chatting affably, discussing the merits of cycling versus motoring, while Percy gave the final touches to the bonnet of Dixie's car.

'Look here,' said Dixie. 'I wonder if you'd care to join us sometime on a little trip around Didsworth in my car? I can see that you're a born cyclist, but perhaps we could take you further afield? There are some very picturesque views in the area.'

'Thanks, that's very kind of you,' Dean said. 'But I prefer to stick with my bike. It's far better exercise. Driving is all very well for older people, but it doesn't keep you fit, does it?'

And with that he was off, leaving Dixie and Percy staring at his disappearing form.

After this Dixie and Percy often caught sight of Dean speeding up the road, off on some new adventure.

One morning, when Percy dropped in on Dixie to see if they might plan another car outing soon,

he found Dixie in his shorts, doing exercises.

'That looks very energetic!' he said. 'Well done, old chap!'

Dixie paused, panting. He was very red in the face.

'Do you know, Percy,' he said, 'I think I may have put on a bit of weight recently. My waistline seems to have increased, and I can't do up the bottom button of my waistcoat. I've decided some-thing has to be done about it.'

'You could go on a diet,' Percy suggested. 'And cut out all those afternoon teas we've been having recently at the cottage creamery.'

'Hmm. Yes. But I don't think that's enough. I think Dean is right. Just driving everywhere in the car means I'm not getting enough exercise. As a matter of fact, I'm thinking of taking up cycling.'

Percy was amazed. 'But you haven't ridden a bicycle in years!' he said. 'Your old one is in the shed with flat tyres.'

'I know. But I'm going to invest in a new one. Something really up to date. And – well, Percy, I'm wondering if it shouldn't be a tandem.'

But there are races, scrapes,
and bumps in the road ahead
for Dixie and Percy.

**What will happen when they
take to two wheels?**

Find out in

DIXIE O'DAY
On His Bike!